My Weird School Special

No More School, April Fools!

Pictures by
Jim Paillot

Dan Gutman

HARPER
An Imprint of HarperCollinsPublishers

To Emma

My Weird School Special: No More School, April Fools!
Text copyright © 2024 by Dan Gutman
Illustrations copyright © 2024 by Jim Paillot
All rights reserved. Printed in the United States of America.

Library of Congress Control Number: 2023936860
ISBN 978-0-06-329009-9 (pbk bdg) — ISBN 978-0-06-329010-5 (trade bdg)

23 24 25 26 27 LBC 5 4 3 2 1
First Edition

Contents

Miss Banks Pulls Another Prank

My name is A.J. and I know what you're thinking. You're thinking about snakes. Because that's what I'm thinking about.

I saw a picture of a snake that swallowed a whole bunny. You could see the shape of the bunny in the middle of the snake! It was gross. I've heard that snakes can swallow alligators, pigs, and even *cows*. Do you think a snake could swallow a kid? I don't want to be that kid. I'm afraid of snakes.

My point is: it was Friday morning. Miss Banks walked into class with a smile on her face.

"Good morning, students!" she said. "It's time to mold young minds!"

"Ugh! Disgusting!" I shouted.

I don't want my mind molded. If you want to mold something, get a tub of Play-Doh.

"Do you know what today is?" asked Miss Banks.

"What's today?" asked Ryan, who will eat anything, even stuff that isn't food.

"It's National Standing Day!" said Miss Banks.

"National Standing Day?" asked Alexia, this girl who rides a skateboard all the time. "What's that?"

"It's a day when we celebrate standing," Miss Banks replied.

"I never heard of National Standing Day," whispered Andrea Young, this annoying girl with curly brown hair.

"Me neither," whispered Emily, who never hears about anything unless Andrea hears about it first.

"Everybody, get out of your seats and stand up," said Miss Banks.

We got out of our seats and stood up. We pledged the allegiance. We did Word of the Day. Miss Banks told us to keep standing to celebrate National Standing

Day. So we did math standing up. Then we did social studies standing up.

I was getting tired of standing up. It felt like we were standing for a million hundred hours.

"Can we sit down now?" asked Michael, who never ties his shoes.

"No," said Miss Banks.

"Do we have to stand up *all day*?" asked Neil, who we call the nude kid even though he wears clothes.

"Of course!" replied Miss Banks. "National Standing Day goes on all day long. It's a national holiday."

"I think it's a *dumb* holiday," I said. "They don't have National Kneeling Day or National Leaning Against a Wall Day."

Actually, those holidays would be cool. But Miss Banks came over to my desk. She looked mad. I thought she might send me to the principal's office.

But suddenly, Miss Banks broke out in a big grin.

"Just kidding!" she said. "There's no such thing as National Standing Day. You can all sit down now."

WHAT?!

Miss Banks pulls lots of pranks.*

"Ha-ha-ha!" she said, laughing her head off. "I got you good! Time is fun when you're having flies!"

Grrrrrr.

---

*Hey, that would make a good book title!

Payback Time

We were on the playground at recess, hanging on the monkey bars. Why do they call them monkey bars? I've never seen any monkeys in the playground. Anyway, we were all pretty mad about what happened in Chapter 1.

"I can't believe Miss Banks got us *again*," said Ryan.

"She's always pulling pranks on us," said Michael.

"And we always fall for them," said Neil.

"Miss Banks is mean," said Alexia. "We're not gonna take it!"

"Do you know what we should do?" asked Andrea. "We should pull a prank on Miss Banks."

"That's right," said Emily, who always thinks Andrea is right.

I was surprised that Andrea wanted to pull a prank on Miss Banks. Andrea *never* breaks the rules. She never does *anything* that might get herself in trouble or prevent her from getting into Harvard someday. Andrea must have been pretty mad about Miss Banks's constant pranking.

"It's payback time," Alexia said. "What prank should we pull on Miss Banks?"

"How about we tell her it's National *Sitting* Day?" suggested Neil. "So we can sit down for the rest of the day."

"We sit down *every* day," Andrea pointed out.

"How about we put bubble wrap under the rug?" suggested Ryan. "So when she

steps on it, it'll pop and freak her out."

"She already did that to *us*," said Andrea. "Remember?"

"How about we let the air out of the tires on her car?" suggested Michael.

"That might be illegal," Ryan said. "We could go to jail."

"I don't *want* to go to jail!" whined Emily. She looked like she might start crying, as usual.

"Nobody's going to jail," Andrea assured Emily.

We needed to come up with the perfect prank. We needed a prank that would get Miss Banks good but wouldn't put us in jail.

We thought and thought and thought.

I thought so hard, I thought my brain was going to explode. That's when I came up with the greatest prank in the history of the world.

"I have an idea!" I whispered, so nobody else would hear. "When Miss Banks goes to write something on the board, we should all turn our chairs and desks around so we're facing the back of the room. That would be hilarious."

"Actually, that's not a bad idea," said Andrea.

"Oooooh!" Ryan said. "Andrea likes A.J.'s idea. They must be in LOVE!"

"When are you gonna get married?" asked Michael.

If those guys weren't my best friends, I

would hate them.

"Miss Banks will be totally surprised," said Neil.

I should get the Nobel Prize for my great idea. That's a prize they give out to people who don't have bells.

After recess, we went back to the classroom and took our seats. We were all giggling in anticipation of our great prank.

"This afternoon," Miss Banks told us, "we're going to learn about the digestive system. It includes the parts of the body that turn food and liquids into the fuel our bodies need *blah blah blah blah . . .*"

She went on and on. We waited for her to write on the board so we could turn our chairs and desks around.

"The parts of the digestive system," continued Miss Banks, "are the mouth, the esophagus, the stomach, the intestines, and *blah blah blah blah . . .*"

The digestive system is really gross. I waited for Miss Banks to turn around and draw a picture of a stomach or something on the whiteboard. But she didn't do it! She just kept talking. It felt like we were waiting a million hundred hours.

Finally, Miss Banks looked at her watch and told us she had to step out of the room for a minute.

"Now!" I shouted as soon as she walked out the front door of the class.

We all rushed to turn our desks and chairs around until we were facing the back of the room. Everybody was giggling.

"This is gonna be *great*," whispered Alexia.

That's when the weirdest thing in the history of the world happened. The *back* door of the classroom opened, and Miss Banks walked in.

"As I was saying," she said, "the first stage of the digestive process is chewing.

When you chew food, it gets broken into smaller pieces and *blah blah blah blah . . ."*

WHAT?! She just went on talking about the yucky digestive system as if we hadn't pulled off the greatest prank in the history of pranks! She turned our prank around and pranked *us*!

Then something even *weirder* happened. The *front* door of the classroom opened and our principal, Mrs. Stoker, walked in. She looked around and saw us all facing the wrong direction, with Miss Banks teaching from the back of the room.

"What's going on?" asked Mrs. Stoker.

"Oh," said Miss Banks, "I stepped out of the room for a moment, and the students turned their desks around. So I thought

I'd teach them from the back of the room."

"We were trying to prank her," admitted Andrea.

"But she pranked us instead," muttered Neil.

Mrs. Stoker shook her head, sighed, and walked out of the room. A few minutes later, an announcement came over the loudspeaker.

"All fourth-grade classes, report to the all-porpoise room."*

Uh-oh.

"We're in trouble now," said Ryan.

---

*I don't know why they call it the all-porpoise room. There are no dolphins in there.

17

A Teachable Moment

Before she was our principal, Mrs. Stoker was a stand-up comedian.* She's always cracking jokes. But not *this* time. When we got to the all-porpoise room, she was standing on the stage with a serious look on her face.

---

*You can read about it in a book called *Mrs. Stoker Is a Joker!*

Everybody was buzzing. But not like bees. That would be weird. I knew what Mrs. Stoker was going to tell us. She was going to say that pulling pranks can be dangerous. Somebody could get hurt. Stuff like that. Grown-ups hate it when kids pull pranks.

"We might get suspended," said Neil.

"She's going to hang us upside down?" I asked.

"No, dumbhead!" said Neil. "We might get kicked out of school."

Oh. I knew that.

Mrs. Stoker held up her hand and made a peace sign, which means shut up.

"Simmer down," she said. We simmered down.

"It has come to my attention . . ." she began.

Uh-oh. Anytime a grown-up says something has come to their attention, you *know* you did something wrong. That's the first rule of being a kid.

"It has come to my attention that the fourth graders like to pull pranks on their teacher."

"Here it comes," whispered Alexia. "We're going to jail."

"And I want to tell you," continued Mrs. Stoker, "that I think that's *great*!"

WHAT?!

"You *liked* our prank?" I shouted.

20

"Yes!" replied Mrs. Stoker. "You kids thought about your prank. You planned it out. You worked together as a group. You used critical thinking skills and *blah blah blah blah*. This as a teachable moment!"

Ugh. Grown-ups *love* teachable moments.

"You kids have given me an idea," continued Mrs. Stoker. "April Fools' Day is next Friday. To celebrate, we're going to have a weeklong contest between the students and the teachers at Ella Mentry School to see who can pull the best pranks. We'll call it . . . The Prank War!"

Everybody started buzzing again. Having a prank war sounded like a great idea. I started thinking about all the pranks we could pull on Miss Banks. This was going to be fun!

But then I remembered something. Teachable moments are *never* fun. They're just another way for grown-ups to trick us into learning stuff. What a scam!

"What's in it for us?" I shouted.

"Well," said Mrs. Stoker, "if you students win The Prank War, we'll have a big candy party! What do you say to *that*?"

"YAY!" we all shouted, which is YAY backward.

"And if the teachers win The Prank War," said Mrs. Stoker, "they'll get a hot tub for the teachers' lounge."

"WOW!" all the teachers shouted, which is MOM upside down.

"And to get everybody into the spirit of The Prank War," said Mrs. Stoker, "on April Fools' Day, I will wear a fake nose and glasses."

A fake nose and glasses? That sounded kind of lame to me.

"That's *all* you're gonna do?" somebody shouted.

"Yes," said Mrs. Stoker. "It will be funny."

Not to *me*. Our old principal, Mr. Klutz, used to do *cool* stuff to get us into the spirit of things.

"You should paint your head orange," shouted Michael. "Mr. Klutz did that one time."

"Remember when he climbed up the flagpole?" asked Neil. "He hung there upside down dressed like Uncle Sam."

"That was hilarious," said Ryan. "Remember when he kissed a pig on the lips?"

Mr. Klutz was nuts. One time he married a turkey. That was before he retired.

"He was so funny," whispered Andrea. "Mrs. Stoker could never fill his shoes."

HUH? That's also HUH backward. Why would you want to fill somebody's shoes? What would you fill them with, anyway?

Everybody was buzzing, until Mrs. Stoker told us to simmer down.

"I'm sorry," she said, "but I'm not Mr. Klutz. And I'm not doing any of those things."

"BOOOOOOOOOO!" Everybody started booing.

"Well, what do you want me to do?" Mrs. Stoker asked.

"You could sit in a shopping cart like a baby, and we could push you around the school," suggested Neil.

"I'm not doing that," said Mrs. Stoker.

"You could see how many hot dogs you can eat in five minutes," suggested Michael.

"I'm not doing that either," said Mrs. Stoker.

"You could dye your hair green," suggested Alexia.

"No *way* I'm doing that," said Mrs. Stoker.

"You don't want to do *anything* fun," somebody shouted. "You're no fun at all."

"NO FUN AT ALL!" everybody started chanting. "NO FUN AT ALL!"

Chanting is cool. It almost doesn't matter *what* you chant.

"Hey, I'm fun!" Mrs. Stoker insisted. "I'm *lots* of fun! I'm a comedian! How about I tell you a few jokes to show you how much fun I am?"

"NO!" everybody shouted. Mrs. Stoker's jokes are terrible.

"If you were *really* fun," I said, "you would bungee jump off the roof while wearing a pink tutu. *That* would get us into the spirit of The Prank War."

"Yeah!" everybody agreed.

"BUN-GEE! BUN-GEE! BUN-GEE!" everybody chanted.

Mrs. Stoker took a deep breath and let out a sigh.

"Okay," she finally agreed. "I'll *do* it!"

"YAY!"

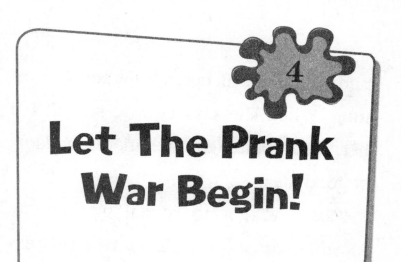

Let The Prank War Begin!

Over the weekend, we got together to think of some cool pranks to pull on Miss Banks. Ryan said we should glue some coins to the floor and watch when she tries to pick them up. Neil said we should put confetti in her umbrella so when she opens it, the confetti will go flying all over. Michael said we should call her cell phone and ask if her refrigerator is running. When she says yes, we should tell her, "You'd better go catch it!" We had lots of good ideas.

When we got to school on Monday morning, there was a big whiteboard next to the front office. It looked like a scoreboard, with Teachers on the left side and Students on the right side.

The gang and I were walking down the hallway to class when we saw Miss Banks.

"Are you kids ready for The Prank War?" she asked us.

"Oh, yeah," I replied. "The teachers are going *down*!"

"I don't *think* so," said Miss Banks. "I was talking with some of the other teachers

over the weekend, and we *really* want that hot tub."

"Well, you're not gonna get it," Ryan told her. "The teachers are old and tired. We're kids, so we're young and full of energy."

"Yeah," added Michael, "and we can't delay our gratification."

Miss Banks stopped and turned to us.

"You think some snot-nosed kids are going to beat the teachers?" she asked. "No way! We've had *years* of experience pulling pranks on kids."

"Yeah, *hundreds* of years," I added.

"Oh, snap!" said Ryan.

"May the better team win," Miss Banks replied.

Principal Stoker was walking right behind us, and I guess she heard what we were saying.

"Enough trash talk," she told us. "We still have to do our regular schoolwork this week. Don't forget that."

We walked into our classroom. Everybody put their backpacks in their cubbies.

"Before we start The Prank War," said Miss Banks, "who wants a piece of sponge cake?"

"I do!"

"I do!"

"I do!"

In case you were wondering, *everybody* wanted sponge cake. Of *course*! Sponge cake is my favorite kind of cake. Miss Banks handed out paper plates and napkins to all of us and opened a cake box on her desk. I was about to take a piece of cake. Then I stopped.

"Hey, wait a minute," I said. "I remember the time you offered us brownies. But you didn't have any brownies. You had a plate with brown letter *E*'s cut out of paper! You said they were brownies. So no thanks. I don't want any sponge cake."

"That's right," said Alexia. "You also offered us doughnuts, but it turned out that they were veggies."

"Yeah, we're not falling for *that* old trick again," said Andrea. "Nice try."

"Suit yourself," Miss Banks told us. "That just means more sponge cake for *me*."

She put a piece of sponge cake on a plate and started eating it.* She closed her eyes and sighed.

"Yummmmm!" she said. "I *lovvvvvvvve* sponge cake."

So do I. Watching Miss Banks eat, I could almost taste the sponge cake.

---

*The cake, that is. It would be weird to eat a plate.

"It sure *looks* like sponge cake," said Emily.

Emily was right. The cake looked like real sponge cake, and it looked *delicious*. It had pink icing and sprinkles on top. My mouth was watering.

But not really. How would you water a mouth?

"There's gotta be a trick," said Michael.

"She's pranking us again."

"What trick?" Miss Banks asked as she took another bite of sponge cake. "Look at it. Smell it."

"Do you *promise* that this is sponge cake?" asked Andrea.

"I promise," said Miss Banks. "It's one hundred percent real, genuine sponge cake."

"Well . . . okay," I said.

Miss Banks put pieces of sponge cake on paper plates and passed them around.

I picked up the sponge cake.

I bit into the sponge cake.

Ugh! It was *horrible*! I couldn't even chew it. I spit a mouthful of icing out on my plate.

"What *is* this?" I asked, wiping my mouth.

"I already told you," said Miss Banks. "It's sponge cake! It's a cake—made out of sponges! Get it? Sponge cake? Ha-ha-ha! Oh, I got you good!"

She pranked us *again*!

While we were spitting out the awful sponge cake, Miss Banks called the front office on the intercom.

"Put it up on the scoreboard, Mrs. Stoker!" she shouted. "I just scored a point for the teachers!"

Grrrrrrr.

I thought Ryan might actually eat Miss Banks's fake sponge cake. He'll eat *any-thing*.

"Wait a minute," said Andrea. "If your sponge cake is just cake made out of sponges, what were *you* eating? I saw you swallow it!"

"Oh," said Miss Banks. "I got one piece of *regular* sponge cake for myself and just made *your* pieces out of sponges."

"Not fair!" shouted Neil.

"You're a *teacher*!" said Alexia. "When a teacher tells us something, we believe it."

Everybody was upset that Miss Banks had pranked us again. That's when the weirdest thing in the history of the world happened.

But I'm not going to tell you what it was.

Okay, okay, I'll tell you. But you have to read the next chapter. So nah-nah-nah boo-boo on you!

Brrrrriinnnnnggggg!

Suddenly, a bell in the hallway started ringing, really loud. The bell in our school sounds like the word "bring." Nobody knows why.

Brrrrriinnnnnggggg! Everybody was alarmed.*

"It must be a fire drill," said Andrea. "We

---

*That's why they call it an alarm.

need to walk outside in single file."

"It can't be a fire drill," said Miss Banks. "They always tell the teachers in advance when there's going to be a fire drill, so we don't schedule a test at that time."

"Maybe it's a tornado drill," suggested Ryan. Every so often we have a tornado drill.

"No, it's not a tornado drill," said Miss Banks.

Brrrrriinnnngggggg!

Then our librarian, Mrs. Roopy, poked her head into the doorway.

"Flood drill!" she shouted. Next she went down the hall shouting to all the other classes, "Flood drill! Flood drill!"

I never heard of a flood drill.

"Flash floods can be very dangerous," said Andrea, who thinks she knows everything. "I saw an article that said you can't see a flash flood coming until it's right on top of you. Then it's too late."

Brrrrriinnnnnggggg!

"Andrea's right," said Miss Banks. "Everybody, take off your shoes and socks, then roll up your pants legs."

Brrrrriiinnngg!

We all rushed to take off our shoes and socks.

"Grab a notebook and climb up on your desk," said Miss Banks. "The water might get high in here. If it's a big wave, ride your desk like a surfboard. You can use your notebook as a paddle."

I grabbed my notebook and climbed up on my desk. Miss Banks got a box of straws from her drawer gave a straw to each of us.

"If the water is over your head," she said, "you can breathe through the straw like a snorkel. Put it in your mouth."

That was pretty smart, I had to admit. The bell stopped ringing. And you'll never believe who walked into the door

at that moment.

Nobody! It would hurt if you walked into a door! But you'll never believe who walked into the door*way.*

It was Mrs. Stoker!

"Why are you all standing on your desks?" she asked. "And what's with the straws?"

"It's a flood drill," I told her.

"We're going to ride our desks like surfboards," said Michael, "and breathe through straws if the water is over our head."

Mrs. Stoker slapped her knees and doubled over laughing.

"There's no such thing as a flood drill," she told us. "That's hilarious!"

"I got you kids *again*!" shouted Miss Banks. "Ha-ha-ha! I can't believe you fell for it! That's the oldest prank in the book!"

"I'll put another point on the scoreboard for the teachers," said Mrs. Stoker.

Grrrrrrr.

She's Gonna Freak Out!

The score was 2–0. The teachers were winning, but there was plenty of time for us to catch up. After school, we didn't go right home. We snuck out to the playground to plan a strategy. We had to think up some great pranks to pull on Miss Banks or we'd never get a candy party.

"Okay," said Andrea, "let's put our heads together."

"I'm not putting my head next to your head," I told Andrea.

"It's just an expression, Arlo!" said Andrea, who calls me by my real name because she knows I don't like it.

"Can you two stop arguing for once?" asked Alexia. "We have bigger fish to fry."

Huh? I was going to ask Alexia what fish had to do with anything, but we had more important things to worry about. Like coming up with great pranks to pull on Miss Banks.

"What if we wrapped up her cell phone with rubber bands?" suggested Michael.

"*Bor . . . ring,*" I groaned.

"What if we stuck Post-it notes all over her car?" suggested Ryan.

"Nah," I muttered.

"What if we put an Out of Order sign on the door to the teachers' bathroom?" said Neil.

"Snoozefest," I said. They were a bunch of dumb ideas.

"Is Miss Banks afraid of anything?" asked Alexia.

"Bugs," Neil said. "Remember when she told us how much she hates insects?"

"Yeah."

"I have an idea!" said Andrea, all excited. "I could make some bugs out of chocolate, and we can put them on her desk when she's not looking!"

"You know how to make chocolate bugs?" Alexia asked.

"Sure," Andrea replied. "I took a baking class after school. They taught us how to make all *kinds* of things out of chocolate."

Of *course*. Andrea takes classes in *every-thing* after school.*

"That's a great idea!" said Emily, who

*If they gave a class on how to clean your bellybutton, she would take that class so she could get better at it.

thinks all Andrea's ideas are great.

But for once in her life, Emily was right. Putting chocolate bugs on Miss Banks's desk *was* a great idea. If she's really afraid of insects, she'll probably jump three feet in the air when she sees her desk covered with them.

We rushed to get to school early on Tuesday morning so we would be in class before Miss Banks showed up. Andrea brought a box filled with chocolate cockroaches, spiders, flies, and ants. They looked really real! Everybody was giggling as we spread the bugs out on Miss Banks's desk.

"She's gonna freak out when she sees *this*!" said Michael.

"It's gonna be great!" said Ryan, rubbing his hands together.

"Finally, the shoe will be on the other foot," said Alexia.

Huh? What did shoes have to do with anything? Why is everybody always talking about shoes?

We put our backpacks in our cubbies and rushed to our seats. I couldn't wait to see the look on Miss Banks's face when she saw bugs crawling on her desk.

A few minutes later, she came into the classroom.

"Good morning!" she said.

She hung up her coat.

She opened the window.

She looked at the clock.

The suspense was killing me!

Finally, Miss Banks went over to her desk.

"Oh, look!" she said. "I *love* chocolate bugs! Time is fun when you're having flies!"

Then she popped some bugs in her mouth.

Grrrrrrr.

The Secret Swimming Pool

We tried *everything* to prank Miss Banks. We put signs on both classroom doors that said Door Is Broken. Use Other Door. She just climbed in through the window. We tried to play "The Why Game." That's when you keep asking "Why?" whenever a grown-up says anything. But Miss Banks played "The Because Game" right back at us.

Every time we tried to pull a prank on Miss Banks, she would pull one on us instead. The other fourth-grade classes weren't doing much better. By lunchtime on Wednesday, the scoreboard near the front office said Teachers 12–Students 4.

The teachers were clobbering us! We needed to do something . . . and fast. We were running out of time. During lunch period, we held an emergency meeting in the vomitorium.

"We should pull a prank with balloons," suggested Andrea.

"No, snakes," Michael said. "Like, we could put a snake in Miss Banks's desk drawer. That would totally freak her out."

"I hate snakes," I said.

"Where would we get snakes, anyway?" asked Alexia.

"From Rent-A-Snake," said Ryan. "You can rent anything."

"Balloons!" insisted Andrea.

"Snakes!" insisted Michael.

Lunch period was over, and we couldn't agree on a prank. We went back to class. That's when the weirdest thing in the history of the world happened. Miss Banks walked into the room.

Well, that's not the weird part because Miss Banks walks into the room all the time. The weird part was what she was wearing . . . a bathing suit!

WHAT?!

"Why are you wearing a bathing suit, Miss Banks?" asked Emily.

"Oh," Miss Banks replied as she dried her hair with a towel. "I just got back from a swim."

"Where did you go swimming?" asked Andrea.

"In the teachers' lounge," she replied.

WHAT?!

"There's a swimming pool in the teachers' lounge?" Neil asked.

"Didn't anybody tell you?" said Miss Banks. "It was installed over the summer."

I thought about that. Was there *really* a swimming pool in the teachers' lounge, or was Miss Banks just pranking us again?

"There's no swimming pool in the teachers' lounge," insisted Alexia.

"Sure there is," said Miss Banks. "We swim laps and play water polo after you kids go home every day. That's why we want to win the hot tub. It would feel so good to come out of the swimming pool and get into a hot tub."

Well, she was right about that. Hot tubs are great.

It was time to go to fizz ed, so we walked a million hundred miles to the gym. When we passed the art room, our art teacher, Ms. Hannah, was wearing a bathing suit too. And she was holding a beach ball.

When we passed by the music room, our music teacher, Mr. Loring, was wearing a bathing suit and flip-flops, and was holding a boogie board. And there was a clothesline outside the music room with towels and goggles hanging on it.

"Hi, Mr. Loring," Miss Banks said as we passed him.

"Hello, Miss Banks," he replied. "Are you coming to the staff pool party after school today?"

"You bet!" said Miss Banks.

This was getting weird.

"Hey," whispered Ryan, "maybe there *is* a swimming pool in the teachers' lounge."

"How come the teachers get a swimming pool and we don't?" whispered Neil. "It's not fair!"

"That's ridorkulous!" whispered Andrea. "*Nobody* has a swimming pool! They're just trying to prank us again."

"You've never been inside the teachers' lounge," Alexia said to Andrea. "You don't know for sure. Maybe they *do* have a swimming pool."

"There's one way to find out," I whispered. "We should sneak into the teachers' lounge after school."

"Yeah!"

When the dismissal bell rang, we got our backpacks and said goodbye to Miss Banks. But instead of going home, we hid behind the back door to the school. I put a rock next to the door so it wouldn't close and lock behind us.

We waited a few minutes, and then we snuck back inside the school. We slinked down the hall, hugging the walls like secret agents.*

"Follow me," I said.

"Shhhhhhhh!" said Alexia.

"We should synchronize our watches," whispered Michael. "That's what secret

---

*Slinking around like a secret agent is cool. You should try it.

agents do in the movies."

"I don't have a watch," Neil whispered.

"*None* of us have watches," whispered Emily.

"*Shhhhhhhh!*" said Alexia.

Finally, we reached the teachers' lounge.

"This will prove once and for all that there's no swimming pool in here," Andrea whispered.

A sign on the door to the teachers' lounge said POOL PARTY TODAY AT 3 P.M.

I looked up and down the hallway.

"The coast is clear," I whispered. "Let's go."

I put my hand on the doorknob.

"Don't open that door!" Michael whispered urgently.

"Why not?" I whispered back.

"In horror movies," whispered Michael, "whenever somebody opens a door, a monster jumps out and kills everybody."

"This isn't a horror movie,"

TEACHERS' LOUNGE

POOL PARTY TODAY AT 3 P.M.

Alexia told Michael. "Chill."

I opened the door a crack. It was completely dark inside the teachers' lounge.

"Turn the light on," whispered Andrea.

"I don't know where the switch—"

I didn't get the chance to finish my sentence because the weirdest thing in the history of the world happened. Something fell on my head! A *bunch* of things fell on my head!

"Snakes!" I screamed. "They're going to eat me!"

Ugh! There were slimy, disgusting snakes all over me! I thought I was gonna die!

"Eeeeeeeek!" screamed Emily.

"Help!" screamed Alexia.

"Run for your lives!" screamed Neil.

We were all yelling and screaming and freaking out. That's when I realized something.

The snakes were fakes!

A light went on inside the teachers' lounge. I looked around the room. Miss Banks was in there. So were Mrs. Roopy, Mr. Loring, Ms. Hannah, and a few other teachers. They were sitting there drinking coffee, which is what grown-ups always do when they're sitting around. Nobody knows why.

"Ha-ha-ha!" shouted Miss Banks. "We got you *again*! That's another point for the teachers!"

Grrrrrrr.

The Prank
Hall of Fame

When I got home from school, I told my parents the teachers were clobbering us in The Prank War. It looked like we were going to lose for sure. That meant no candy party, and the teachers would get a hot tub. Bummer in the summer!

"It's not fair!" I complained.

"Why don't you go to Goofy Gifts?" my

dad suggested. "It has all kinds of silly stuff. Maybe they have some things that will help you pull pranks on Miss Banks."

Of *course*! Goofy Gifts is a store that sells goofy gifts, so it has the perfect name.

"Didn't somebody give you a Goofy Gifts gift card for your birthday?" asked my mom.

That's *right*! My aunt gave me a twenty-five-dollar gift card! I forgot all about it.

I called up Ryan and we went to Goofy Gifts together. It's a really big store, and they sell all kinds of junk. We walked around for a while, until I saw a wall filled with silly gifts like whoopie cushions, sneezing powder, and joy buzzers. It was *amazing*! They even had lollipops shaped like poop. They were called Lollipoops.

"Look at all this great stuff!" marveled Ryan. "It might as well be the Prank Hall of Fame."

"This is gonna score us *tons* of points," I told him. "We're sure to win The Prank War now!"

We had twenty-five dollars to spend. The prank gifts were pretty cheap, so we could get a bunch of them. I got a shopping basket. Ryan put some itching powder in the basket. I put in a can of fart spray. Ryan put in a dribble glass and a bag of Lollipoops. I put in some fake ice cubes with bugs inside them and a stink bomb. We also threw in some fake mustaches, a squirting calculator, a skunk-scented candle, and a can of dehydrated water.*

Ryan picked up a rubber chicken.

"What are you gonna do with *that*?" I asked him.

"I don't know," he replied. "You can always use a rubber chicken."

We totaled up our stuff. It was exactly

---

*To make water, you just add water.

twenty-five dollars.

"This is gonna be *great*!" Ryan said as we got in line to pay.

"We're gonna get Miss Banks *good*!" I replied.

The line was long, but they had a bunch of cashiers, so it moved fast. Soon we were at the front of the line.

"Next customer!" a lady shouted.

And you'll never believe in a million hundred years who was standing behind the cash register.

It was Miss Banks!

NOOOOOOOOOOOOO!

"Quick," I whispered to Ryan. "Hide the basket!"

"*You* hide the basket!" Ryan whispered.

"I can't hide the basket!" I whispered back. "Let's make a run for—"

But I didn't get the chance to finish my sentence because Miss Banks spotted us. This was the worst thing to happen since TV Turnoff Week! I wanted to run away to Antarctica and go live with the penguins.

"A.J.! Ryan!" she said. "What are you boys doing here?"

I tried to hide the basket behind my back, but the bag of Lollipoops fell on the floor. I didn't know what to say. I didn't know what to do. I had to think fast.

"Oh, nothing," I replied. "What are *you* doing here, Miss Banks?"

"I work here after school," she told us. "It's hard to make ends meet on a teacher's salary. Did you want to buy those Lolli-poops? They're on sale today. Buy one, get one free."

"Uh, no thanks," Ryan said. "We just stopped by to . . . say hello."

"Yeah, hello," I said.

"I'll see you boys at school tomorrow," said Miss Banks. "Next customer!"

We put the prank stuff back on the shelf and ran out of there.

The next day would be Friday—April Fools' Day. The *last* day of The Prank War. I went to bed desperately trying to think up pranks to pull on Miss Banks. I thought and thought and thought, until I thought my brain would explode. Finally, I fell asleep.

April Fools' Day

When we walked into class on Friday morning, the bell in the hallway started ringing.

Brrrrrriinnnnngggggg!

"Oh no!" shouted Miss Banks. "It's a flood drill! Quick! Everybody, take off your shoes and socks!"

"Very funny," said Alexia.

"No, I *mean* it!" shouted Miss Banks. "It might be a *real* flash flood this time!"

"Yeah, right," I scoffed.

Brrrrrriinnnnngggggg!

"Hurry!" yelled Miss Banks. "Roll up your pants legs! Grab your notebooks and climb up on your desks!"

"Forget it," said Ryan. "We're not falling for that old prank again."

"Yeah," said Andrea. "We weren't born yesterday."

Huh? If we were born yesterday, we would be one day old. Babies don't go to school.

Brrrrrriinnnnnggggggg!

That's when the weirdest thing in the history of the world happened. I looked out the window.

Well, that's not the weird part. I look out the window all the time. The weird part was what I *saw* out the window. It was a wave, a wall of water! And it was coming straight toward the school!

"It *is* a flash flood!" I shouted. "It's not a prank!"

"A.J.'s right!" shouted Neil.

"I'm scared!" yelled Emily.

We were *all* scared. The wall of water rolled across the playground and came shooting through the open windows of our class! Water was pouring into the room.

Brrrrrriinnnnnggggg!

"Run for your lives!" shouted Neil.

"No time for that!" shouted Miss Banks. "Climb on your desks! We'll ride them like surfboards! Use your notebook as a paddle!"

But it was too late. The water was up to my waist now. Books and backpacks were floating all over the room. We would have to swim if we were going to make it out of there alive.

"Everyone, stay calm!" shouted Miss Banks.

"Help!" somebody shouted.

"I *told* you flash floods are dangerous!" Andrea shouted. "You can't see them coming until they're right on top of you!"

"That doesn't matter now!" I shouted.

"We've got to swim out of here! Somebody open the door!"

"Glub-glub," Emily glubbed as her head dipped below the water. "I can't swim!"

"Grab my hand, Emily!" Andrea shouted.

"I'm drowning!" somebody screamed. "I want my mommy!"

"I can't breathe!" shouted Neil. "Where are the straws?"

Everybody was yelling and screaming and freaking out.

Then, suddenly, the alarm stopped ringing. And you'll never believe what happened next.

I woke up.

Ha-ha-ha! None of that stuff happened. I made up the whole chapter! I can't believe you actually fell for it! I got you good! Nah-nah-nah boo-boo on you!*

---

*You got pranked while you were reading a book about pranking!

The Real April Fools' Day

Finally, it was the *real* Friday—April Fools' Day. The Prank War was just about over. The teachers were winning by the score of 15–9. It was hopeless. They would get a hot tub, but we wouldn't be getting a candy party. Bummer in the summer!

All of us were sad. One by one, we trudged into the classroom.

"Congratulations," I grumbled to Miss Banks. "I guess you teachers won The Prank War. Happy April Fools' Day."

"Oh, today isn't April Fools' Day," she replied. "Today is March thirty-second."

WHAT?!

"I didn't know March had thirty-two days," Ryan said as he sat down.

"Oh yes, absolutely," said Miss Banks.

At that moment, our science teacher, Mr. Docker, walked by the room.

"Oh, Mr. Docker!" shouted Miss Banks. "How many days are in March?"

"Thirty-two, of course," he replied. "You see, due to the earth's rotation and the pull of gravity at the equator, we have to add an extra leap day every four years to adjust for the *blah blah blah blah . . ."*

I had no idea what he was talking about. But Mr. Docker knows about science stuff, so he must be right.

"If there are thirty-two days in March," I said, "that means we have *one more day* left in The Prank War! We can still catch up with the teachers and win a candy party!"

"YAY," everybody shouted, which is also YAY backward.

We were all high-fiving each other. The only one who didn't look happy was Andrea.

"Wait a minute!" she said. "I remember the poem we learned in third grade:

Thirty days has September,
April, June, and November.
All the rest have thirty-one,
except February which has—"

"March *doesn't* have thirty-two days!" shouted Neil. "Miss Banks is pranking us again!"

"That means today isn't the thirty-second day of March," yelled Alexia. "It's the first day of April—April Fools' Day!"

"Ha-ha-ha!" laughed Miss Banks. "Got you again!"

"We pranked you good!" said Mr. Docker. "Score another point for the teachers!"

Grrrrrr.

At that moment, an announcement

came over the loudspeaker.

"All fourth-grade classes, report to the all-porpoise room."

We lined up in single file. When we got to the all-porpoise room, Mrs. Stoker was up on the stage. Next to her was the scoreboard:

Teachers 16–Students 9. They had beaten us fair and square.

What a humiliation! No candy party for us. This was the worst thing to happen since National Poetry Month. We were the saddest group of kids in the history of the world.

"Well," said Mrs. Stoker, "The Prank War is over, and the winner is . . . of course . . . the teachers!"

"YAY!" shouted all the teachers.

"BOO!" shouted all the kids.

The teachers were hooting and hollering and high-fiving each other like they had just won the Super Bowl.

"Teachers rule, kids drool!" shouted Miss Banks, cupping her hands around her mouth. "Nah-nah-nah boo-boo on you!"

"HOT TUB! HOT TUB! HOT TUB!" the teachers started chanting.

"Teachers can be so immature," said Andrea.

"Okay, simmer down," said Mrs. Stoker. "I have an announcement to make."

Everybody simmered down.

"*All* of you did a great job in The Prank War," said Mrs. Stoker, "so I made a decision. Even though the students lost, we're going to have a candy party anyway!"

WHAT?!

"YAY!"

"I was going to give you kids a candy party no matter *who* won The Prank War," said Mrs. Stoker. "Ha-ha-ha! I pranked you good! Happy April Fools' Day!"

I didn't care if she pranked us. The only thing that mattered was that we were

HOT TUB! HOT TUB!

going to get candy! We were all yelling and screaming and high-fiving each other like we had just won the Super Bowl.

Miss Lazar, our custodian, came out with a wheelbarrow full of candy—Milk Duds and Kit Kats and Snickers and Tootsie Pops and those little bite-size Milky Ways. It was like Halloween. I had never seen so much candy in my life. Miss Lazar passed it out to all the classes.

I unwrapped a Twix bar. *Mmmmm*, it

looked good. I was about to put it in my mouth when I stopped.

"Wait a minute!" I said. "How do we know this candy is *real*?"

"Yeah," said Michael. "It could be fake candy."

"It's probably made out of rubber," said Neil, "or sponge or soap or something like that."

"I'm not eating that fake candy," said Ryan, and he'll eat *anything*. "It's a trick. The teachers are pranking us again."

"Nice try," said Alexia, putting a Snickers back in the wheelbarrow. "But we're not falling for it."

We refused to eat the candy. Mrs. Stoker insisted it was real, but none of us were buying it. The teachers had tricked us so many times. I didn't trust *anybody* anymore.

I looked around and saw kids in other classes gobbling down candy like they hadn't eaten anything in days. They looked really happy.

Hmmm. Maybe it *was* real candy. I took a tiny little nibble of my Twix to see if it was just a potato covered in chocolate. And you know what?

IT WAS REAL!

I took another bite, and another. Then I stuffed my face with as much candy as I could hold. I thought I was gonna throw up. It was the greatest day of my life.

In the middle of the candy party, Andrea stood up, like she had a big announcement to make.

"Well, I guess it's time," she said.

"Time for what?" I asked.

"Time for Mrs. Stoker to bungee jump off the roof of the school while wearing a pink tutu," said Andrea.

That's right! I had forgotten that she was going to do that!

"BUN-GEE! BUN-GEE! BUN-GEE!" we started chanting.

Mrs. Stoker told us to simmer down.

"Everybody, return to your classes," she said, "and get ready for first period."

"But you said you would bungee jump

off the roof of the school while wearing a pink tutu," complained Andrea.

"I don't have a tutu," said Mrs. Stoker, "or a bungee cord."

Ms. Hannah, our art teacher, stood up.

"Here's a tutu," she said, holding it up. "I made it during my free period."

Then Miss Lazar, our custodian, stood up.

"I have the bungee cord all set up on the roof," she said. "It's ready to go."

Everyone was excited to see Mrs. Stoker bungee jump off the roof. Even the teachers were excited.

"BUN-GEE! BUN-GEE! BUN-GEE!" we chanted.

Mrs. Stoker stood there with a frightened look on her face. Then she crossed her arms in front of herself.

"Well, I'm not doing it!" she said. "And that's final."*

The Big Surprise Ending

After all those pranks we pulled on the teachers and all the pranks the teachers pulled on us, I couldn't believe Mrs. Stoker wouldn't bungee jump off the roof in a pink tutu. Everybody was mad, even the teachers.

"But you *promised*!" Alexia shouted. "You're no fun at all."

"NO FUN AT ALL!" everybody started chanting. "NO FUN AT ALL!"

Mrs. Stoker waited until we were finished chanting.

"I was *never* going to bungee jump off the roof," she said. "That was *my* little prank! Ha-ha-ha! I got you good. April Fools!"

"BOOOOOOOOO!"

"That's not fair!" somebody shouted.

"What about the hot tub for the teachers' lounge?" shouted Miss Banks. "Was that a prank too?"

"Of *course*!" said Mrs. Stoker. "Do you have any idea how much a hot tub costs? I don't have the budget for that. We can barely afford pencils."

"BOOOOOOOOO!"

Everybody was *really* mad! Even Andrea had on her mean face. The teachers were shouting. Kids started throwing Milk Duds and Raisinets at Mrs. Stoker. The all-porpoise room was filled with flying candy.

"Not fair!"

"You promised!"

"Cheater!"

Mrs. Stoker shielded her face with her hands and dodged the flying Milk Duds.

"I wouldn't want to be in *her* shoes right now," Ryan told me.

Huh? Why would I *ever* want to be in Mrs. Stoker's shoes? They wouldn't even fit. I like my own shoes. Why is everybody always talking about shoes, anyway?

It looked like a revolution was going on.

Then, suddenly, Mrs. Stoker started to cry.

"I'm afraid of heights," she blubbered.

Everybody stopped yelling and throwing candy. I was mad that Mrs. Stoker broke her promise to us, but I couldn't expect somebody to bungee jump off a roof if they're afraid of heights.

I felt a little sorry for Mrs. Stoker. We all did. Miss Banks went up on the stage and gave her a tissue to dry her eyes.

And you'll never believe who walked

into the door at that moment.

Nobody! You could break your nose walking into a door. I thought we went over that in Chapter 5. But you'll never believe who *opened* the door and walked into the all-porpoise room.

It was Mr. Klutz, our old principal! And he was wearing a pink tutu!

WHAT?! I didn't see *that* coming!

"Mr. Klutz!" shouted Mrs. Stoker. "What are *you* doing here?"

"I came to bungee jump off the roof!" Mr. Klutz announced.

"YAY!" everybody shouted. We really wanted to see *somebody* bungee jump off the roof. It didn't really matter who it was. And Mr. Klutz looked even funnier wearing a pink tutu than Mrs. Stoker would have.

"We miss you, Mr. Klutz!" shouted Andrea.

"I miss you kids too!" he shouted back. "When I heard that today was the last day of The Prank War, I came right over."

"HOORAY FOR MR. KLUTZ!" somebody shouted.

Mrs. Stoker said it wouldn't be safe for so many kids to be up on the roof at the

same time, so we all went out on the front lawn. Mr. Klutz took the stairs up to the roof with Miss Lazar. We waited for them to get up there.

"Mr. Klutz is nuts," Ryan said to me.*

"Yeah, he'll do *anything*," I agreed.

We waited a million hundred seconds. Finally, we saw Mr. Klutz standing on the roof. Miss Lazar helped him strap on the bungee cord. There was electricity in the air.

Well, not really. If there was electricity in the air, we would have been electrocuted. But we were all glued to our seats.

Well, not really. We were just standing on the lawn. Why would anybody glue themself to a seat? How would you get the glue off your pants?

"Are you kids ready?" Mr. Klutz shouted down to us.

---

*Hey, that would make a good book title too!

"Yes!" we shouted back. Then we started chanting, "TEN . . . NINE . . . EIGHT . . . SEVEN . . . SIX . . . FIVE . . . FOUR . . . THREE . . . TWO . . . ONE!"

"Happy April Fools' Day!" Mr. Klutz shouted. And he jumped off the roof.

Well, that's pretty much what happened. You should have *been* there! We got to see it live and in person!

Maybe the teachers will get a hot tub after all. Maybe Mrs. Stoker will sit in a shopping cart like a baby. Maybe Miss Banks will give us some sponge cake that isn't made out of sponges. Maybe people will stop talking about shoes all the time. Maybe we'll see monkeys on the playground. Maybe a snake will swallow a kid. Maybe next April Fools' Day we'll have another Prank War. Maybe I'll ride my desk like a surfboard.

But it won't be easy!

MY WeiRd SchooL SpeciaL

No More School, April Fools!

WEIRD EXTRAS!

★ The History of April Fools' Day

★ Pranks, Pranks, and More Pranks

★ Fun Games and Weird Word Puzzles

★ The World of Dan Gutman Checklist

THE HISTORY
OF APRIL FOOLS' DAY

Hi there, history nerds! This is Professor A.J. and I'm here to tell you about the history of pranks, pranking, and April Fools' Day. You can trust me. I'm a professor, which means I know everything about everything.

Hold your horses, Arlo.

Well, if it isn't Andrea Young, or as I like to call her, the Human Homework Machine.

You're not a professor, Arlo, and you don't know *anything*. I'm here to correct your mistakes.

But, Andrea, as you know, I never make mistakes. I'm infallible. That means I never fall.

We'll see about that.

Okay, it all started back in ancient Egypt with this lady named April—

Stop, Arlo! You totally made that up. Just like you make *everything* up.

Okay, Miss Smarty Pants, then why don't *you* tell everybody how April Fools' Day started?

I can't. Because *nobody* knows how it started! But back in the Middle Ages, some people used to celebrate the new year from March 25 until April 1. People who celebrated the new year on January 1 made fun of the people who were celebrating at the beginning of April.

Anybody who celebrates the new year in April *should* be made fun of.

All we know for sure is that people have been pulling pranks for a *long* time, and especially on the first day of April.

Nobody knows why.

PRANKS, PRANKS, AND MORE PRANKS

PRANKS AROUND THE WORLD

April Fools' Day is celebrated all over the world, from Germany to Turkey, from Iran to Israel, and in Finland, Norway, and Denmark. Sometimes it's called All Fools' Day.

Here's a prank they pull in Ireland—they pick some poor sap and tell him to deliver an "important letter" to some other person. That person reads the letter and tells the poor sap to deliver it to somebody else. Then *they* read it and ask the guy to take it to somebody *else*. When the letter is finally opened by the last person, it says, "Send the fool further."

April 1 is called April Fish Day in Italy, France, Belgium, Switzerland, and Canada. People try to attach a paper fish to their victim's back without being noticed. And in Argentina, Columbia, Belgium, and Spain, people pull pranks on December 28.

If I ever go to Thailand, I'm not going to pull any pranks at *all*. On April Fools' Day in 2021, the police warned that posting fake news could lead to five years in prison.

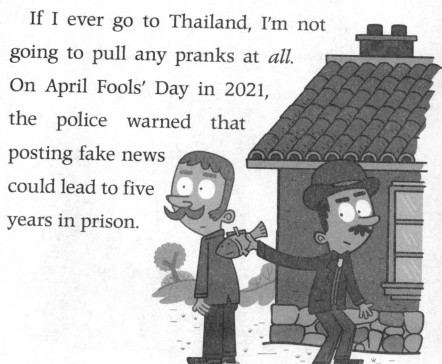

PRANKS FOR THE MEMORIES

Some April Fools' pranks have become famous. Here are just a few I dug up, with no help from Arlo . . .

- In 1938, there was a fake CBS Radio broadcast about aliens from Mars invading New Jersey and wiping out the population with poison gas. It was so convincing that people fled their homes and caused a panic.

- In 1956, a Brazilian candidate named Cacareco got 100,000 votes and won a seat on the city council. The weird thing was that Cacareco a four-year-old rhinoceros in a zoo!
- On April Fools' Day in 1957, the British Broadcasting Corporation reported about farmers harvesting freshly grown spaghetti from a tree in Switzerland. They were flooded with requests from people wanting to buy a spaghetti plant.
- On April Fools' Day in 1965, a London professor announced he had perfected Smellovision—a technology that would transmit smells through TV screens. He did a demonstration with

onions and coffee and told people to stand six feet away from their TV and sniff. Thousands claimed they could smell the aromas. Some even said the onions made their eyes water.

- In 1969, people in the Netherlands were told that inspectors were going to drive around with scanners to find out who had paid their radio and TV tax. To avoid detection, people were told to wrap their radios and TVs with aluminum foil. After that, the supermarkets sold out of aluminum foil.
- On April Fools' Day in 1996, Taco Bell announced it had purchased the Liberty Bell and renamed it the "Taco Liberty Bell."

- On April Fools' Day in 2016, the National Geographic website announced it would no longer publish photos of naked animals.

BECOME A PRANKSTER

Arlo and I pull pranks on each other all the time.

The difference is that my pranks are way better than Andrea's.

Not! We think pulling pranks is fun. I bet it's even good for your health because it relieves stress. But some people think pulling pranks can be rude, creepy, and mean.

Those people need to get a sense of humor transplant. But if you're gonna pull pranks, keep a few things in mind.

Right. Like, it's okay to pull harmless pranks on your good friends and your family, but you shouldn't pull them on strangers.

Yeah, if somebody I didn't know pulled a prank on me, I'd be angry. But if Ryan or Michael pulled the same prank on me, I'd probably think it was funny.

Also, don't pull pranks on people who get upset easily or don't like to be surprised.

You don't want to hurt anybody's feelings or make them think they're being bullied. You want to make them laugh. And of course, you don't want to do anything that's dangerous, will cause damage, or will get you in trouble.

When you're pulling your prank, keep a straight face. Here are some harmless pranks for you to try out . . .

THE CLASSICS

There are lots of classic silly pranks. You can glue a coin to the floor and ask somebody to pick it up. You can tell somebody their shoes are untied or their fly is open. Made you look!

Some stores sell gag products that are great for pranking. You can buy itching powder or sneezing powder. A dribble glass has holes in it so when your victim takes a drink, it spills all over their shirt. You can buy glitter to make a glitter bomb, or you can get a whoopee cushion and hide it under somebody's couch cushions.

FUN WITH FOOD

Food is funny, and there are lots of great food pranks. If you want to get a fast laugh, all you have to do is put sugar in a saltshaker.

Or toothpaste in an Oreo.

Or mayonnaise in an ice-cream sandwich.

Or food coloring in a milk carton. Here's a great prank to play on somebody's birthday: Fill a balloon with water and put it in a cake pan. Decorate the balloon with icing and sprinkles to make it look like a real cake. When the "cake" is cut, the birthday kid better have some towels handy.

You can confuse your parents by putting forks where the spoons are supposed to go and spoons where the forks to go. This will drive them crazy.

While nobody's looking, jam a plastic straw into a marshmallow. Then take the straw out and stick it into somebody's glass. They won't be able to drink anything because their straw is clogged up with marshmallow!

Get a bunch of googly eyes and stick them on the eggs in your refrigerator. When anybody opens the door, they'll see the eggs staring back at them. Googly eyes are funny no matter *what* you stick them on.

I love this one. Hide a raisin in a napkin and hold the napkin in one hand. While somebody is watching, pretend to swat a fly with your other hand. Next, pretend to pick up the dead fly with the napkin. Then, eat the raisin! It will look like you ate a fly! Yuck!

PRANKS TO PULL ON YOUR FRIENDS OR SIBLINGS

Some kids will fall for *anything*. Stuff cotton balls into the toes of your victim's shoes. When they put the shoes on, they'll think their feet grew, or their shoes got smaller.

Pour a little water into your hand while you're right behind somebody. Then fake a loud sneeze and throw the water on the back of the person's neck.

Act all excited and wake up your brother or sister with "It's a snow day! No school!"

Before a family dinner, put a temporary tattoo on your arm. When everybody sits down to eat, tell them you have an announcement to make. Then, without saying anything, roll up your sleeve.

Get the same hat in four sizes. Wear the smallest one when you first see your victim. Then excuse yourself and switch to the next larger hat. After a while, do that again. And *again*. When you have the biggest hat on, your victim will think your head must be shrinking.

Nobody's gonna fall for that.

You'd be surprised. How about this one? Use a marker to write "turn me over" on a smooth, flat rock. On the other side of the rock, write "you just let a rock tell you what to do."

While your victim is sleeping, put a little toothpaste or shaving cream on their fingers. Then tickle their nose.

Or draw the outline of a big bug on a piece

of paper and cut it out with scissors. Tape it to the inside of a lampshade. When your victim turns on the light, it will look like there's a something crawling around inside it.

Bugs are great. Buy some plastic bugs and freeze them into ice cubes. Then put them into somebody's drink. You can also freak people out by putting plastic bugs just about *anywhere* really.

Put confetti on the top of the blades of a ceiling fan. When somebody turns the fan on, they're going to get a shower of confetti.

TOILETS AND UNDERWEAR

There's nothing funnier than underwear. Well, toilets are hilarious too. The classic toilet prank is to pick up the seat and cover the bowl with plastic wrap. Then lower the seat and wait for the fun to begin. That can be kind of gross, of course.

Here's an idea that doesn't require as much cleanup. Tape a small bag of dry pasta to the bottom of a toilet seat. When the next person sits down, *crunch!* They'll think they cracked the seat.

Drop a candy bar into the swimming pool and wait for somebody to spot it. If nobody does, just scream out, "SOMEBODY POOPED IN THE POOL!"

That's gross, Arlo.

What's gross about a candy bar in a swimming pool?

PRANKS TO PULL ON YOUR PARENTS

Attach a rubber band to the nozzle of the kitchen sink sprayer so it's always on. Point the nozzle toward you. When your mom or dad goes to turn on the water, it will shoot all over them.

Do this one when your parents aren't around. Take all the clothes out of your dad's drawers and put them in your mom's drawers. Then put her clothes into his drawers.

Unscrew the cap of your mom's or dad's shampoo bottle. Cover the top of the bottle with a piece of plastic wrap. Then screw the cap back on and trim off any of the plastic wrap that shows. When your mom or dad tries to use the shampoo, nothing comes out!

Get some clear nail polish and paint the bar of soap in your parents' bathroom. When they go to use the soap, it won't lather. This prank also works with pencils.

This is just the beginning. There are loads more pranks you can pull on the people in your life. Go online and search for them. Oh, wait. That's research! Forget I brought it up. Happy April Fools' Day!

FUN GAMES AND
WEIRD WORD PUZZLES

Directions: Help A.J. and Andrea navigate this maze to reach the biggest prank of them all!

HIDDEN WORD HUNT

Directions: Find all twelve April Fools' Day words hidden in this messy jumble of letters.

```
S H O A X J G T Y M M M L G D
I Y P K I K G F B I F Q F D D
N E A D Q V F L T S B A N T G
Q B M B W L G I F C Y L V E U
X N P S H H A O H H T C W G T
W S E H F J G C P I O I A T R
B F P E L O S S T E M V H M I
W Q R N R K L X L F F P T O C
Y R A A I E J A X U O Z C A K
T A N N K K Y K V L O B I P S
Z Q K I P F R F O O L K U R D
S S S G A A F R R Q E K Z I C
N D V A R K Y W J I R P J L Y
V N Y N D E V O D Q Y I H E G
L T B S M W O C S U C K E R W
```

**SHENANIGANS GAGS SUCKER
PRANKS APRIL FOOL TRICKS HOAX
FAKE MISCHIEF JOKE TOMFOOLERY**

KEY

S (H O A X) J G T Y (M) M M L G D
I Y P K I K G F B (I) F Q F D D
N E A D Q V F L T S B A N T G U
Q B M B W L (G) I F C (H) Y L V E U
X N P (S) H H (A) O H I (T) C W G T (T)
W S E (H) F F (G) C P E (O) I A T H (R)
B F (P) (E) L (J) (S) S F (M) V H M O (I)
W Q (R) (N) R (O) L X L F P T O (C)
Y R (A) (A) I (K) J A X U O Z C U (K)
T A (N) (N) K (E) Y K V L B I (A) (S)
Z Q (K) (I) P (F) R (F O O L) K U (P) R D
S S (S) (G) A (A) F R R Q E K Z (R) C Y
N D V (A) R (K) Y W J I R P J (I) C Y
V N Y (N) D (E) V O D Q Y I H (L) E G
L T B (S) M W O C (S U C K E R W)

THE WORLD OF DAN GUTMAN CHECKLIST

MY WEIRD SCHOOL

MY WEIRD SCHOOL DAZE

MY WEIRDER SCHOOL

MY WEIRD SCHOOL SPECIAL

MY WEIRDEST SCHOOL

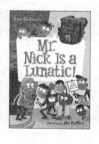

MY WEIRDER-EST SCHOOL

MY WEIRD SCHOOL FAST FACTS

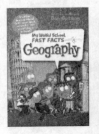

MY WEIRD SCHOOL GRAPHIC NOVELS

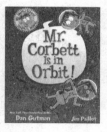

MY WEIRD TIPS

MY WEIRD SCHOOL
JOKES, GAMES, AND PUZZLES

More weird books from Dan Gutman

My Weird School

My Weird School Graphic Novel

My Weirder School

My Weirdest School

My Weirder-est School

My Weirdtastic School

My Weird School Fast Facts

My Weird School Daze

HARPER
An Imprint of HarperCollinsPublishers

harpercollinschildrens.com